miffy on holiday

This book belongs to:

....

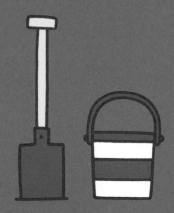

simon and schuster
First published in Great Britain in 2014 by Simon and Schuster UK Ltd
1st Floor, 222 Gray's Inn Road, London WC1X 8HB
A CBS Company
Publication Licensed by Mercis Publishing bv, Amsterdam
Illustrations Dick Bruna © copyright Mercis bv, 1953-2014
Design and text © 2014 Simon and Schuster UK
ISBN 978-1-4711-2213-2
Printed and bound in China
10 9 8 7 6 5 4 3 2 1
www.simonandschuster.co.uk
www.miffy.com

miffy on holiday

SIMON AND SCHUSTER
London New York Sydney Toronto New Delhi

Miffy's daddy and mummy have
something to tell Miffy.

'We are going on holiday!'

Miffy is very excited.
She has never been on holiday before.

Find these stickers and add them to the picture:

Miffy wants to know where they
are going.

'To the seaside!' says Daddy Bunny.
'To play on the beach and swim in
the sea!' says Mummy Bunny.

Find these stickers and add them to the picture:

Miffy is packing her own suitcase.
She packs some pants, a dress
and a pair of shoes.

'I'm ready to go!' says Miffy.

Find these stickers and add them to the picture:

Daddy Bunny drives the car.
It is windy on the way to the seaside.

'I hope it's sunny when we get there,'
says Mummy Bunny.

Find these stickers and add them to the picture:

Miffy's family is staying in a house.
The holiday house is different from
Miffy's house.

Miffy likes the blue door.

Find these stickers and add them to the picture:

The plates in the holiday house are different too, but Mummy Bunny makes Miffy's favourite foods.

'Carrots!' says Miffy.

Find these stickers and add them to the picture:

The bedroom in the holiday house
is different too.
Luckily, Miffy packed her teddy bear.

Miffy falls asleep.

Find these stickers and add them to the picture:

In the morning, Miffy and her parents are at the seaside!

Daddy Bunny has pitched a tent. It has a yellow flag so they remember which tent is theirs.

Find these stickers and add them to the picture:

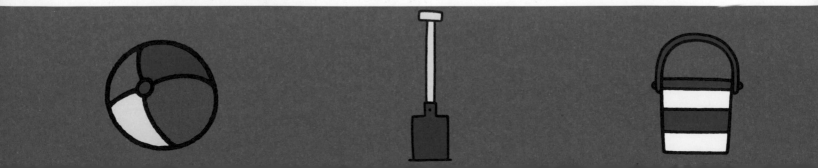

Splish! Splash!

Miffy is swimming in the sea!

The water is nice and cool.

Find these stickers and add them to the picture:

Now Miffy is playing on the beach.

She builds a big wall of sand.

The sand is warm and dry.

Find these stickers and add them to the picture:

Swimming and playing has made Miffy tired.

Miffy and her parents say goodbye to the holiday house and drive home.

Find these stickers and add them to the picture:

Miffy is now in her own house, in her own bed, with her own slippers.
She still has her shells from the seaside.

What a lovely holiday!

Bye-bye!

Find these stickers and add them to the picture: